D0394271

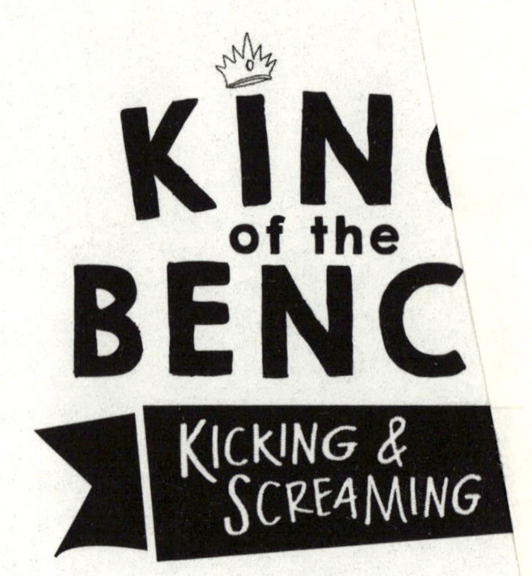
KIN
of the
BENC
KICKING &
SCREAMING

KING of the BENCH

STEVE MOORE

HARPER
An Imprint of HarperCollinsPublishers

King of the Bench: Kicking & Screaming

www.harpercollinschildrens.com

ISBN 978-0-06-220334-2

Typography by Katie Klimowicz

18 19 20 21 22 CG/LSCH 10 9 8 7 6 5 4 3 2 1

❖

First Edition

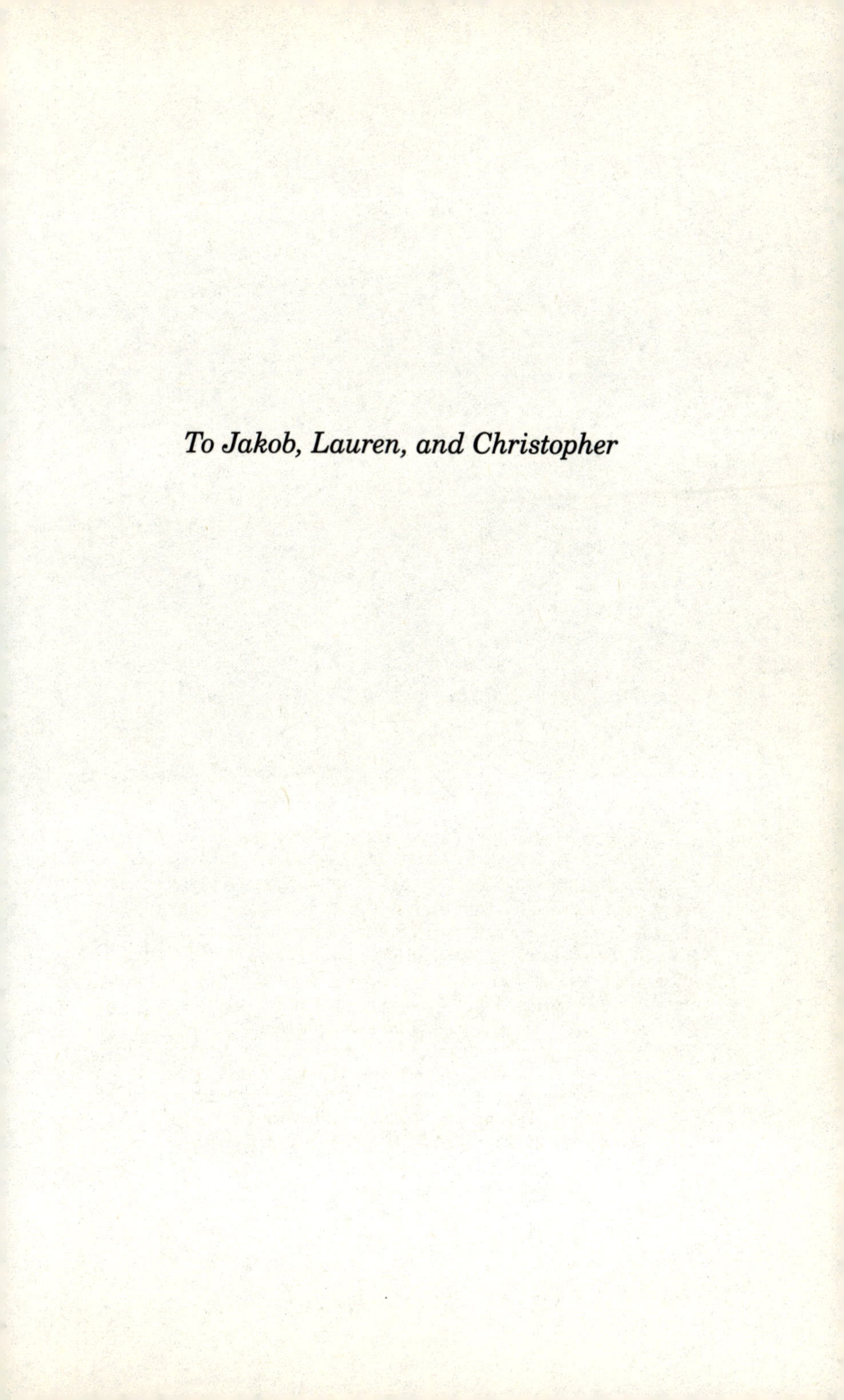

To Jakob, Lauren, and Christopher

PROLOGUE

My name is Steve, and I am a benchwarmer.

In case you don't already know, I love sports. I'm not a hotshot athlete or anything. Not even close. So I only get into games when the score is about a hundred to zip.

And I'm fine with that because I love the other stuff that goes on *around* the games almost as much as playing.

Like when I stick my face in the pocket of a spanking-new baseball glove and take a big whiff of the fresh leather smell.

Or when I put on a football uniform and I look like a gnarly Roman gladiator with a huge chip on his shoulder.

Or when I ride a bus to an away game and pull off all kinds of shenanigans with my friends. (Unless we're sitting in the front seats right next to the coach.)

So I love sports, but I don't love *every* sport. Here are a few examples of sports that don't exactly fry my burger:

But there is one sport that I really dislike, and it's probably the most popular sport in the entire world.

In this book, I'm going to spill my guts about how I blabbed my opinion about that sport and practically ruined a close friendship. And about my embarrassing bodily affliction. And about a kid from Brazil with superhuman athletic skills.

And I'm not even exaggerating.

Right about now you're probably curious.

Stop!

Sorry.

I can't reveal any details right now because—big, drool-y *duh*—it's pretty much a rule when writing a book that you don't just blurt out the juicy plot stuff in the first few pages.

So I'll tell you more when the time is right or I get in the mood. Whichever comes first.

All you need to know for now is that, even though I'm a benchwarmer, I do have some skills.

For example, I have excellent hand-eye coordination.

That's a huge advantage when I dive to catch a baseball inches above the ground. Or when I dribble a basketball. Or when someone in a museum shouts, "Think fast!"

So I'm not a total drooling dweeb, okay? And when it comes to sitting on the bench, I'm probably better at it than anyone else my age in the entire city—maybe the entire world.

End of the pine or middle of the pine, doesn't matter. I pretty much rule the bench.

No brag. It's just a fact.

I'm King of the Bench!

Okay, I'm in the mood now.

I was going to keep you waiting until the suspense built to the point where you couldn't stand it a minute longer, but I'll spill my guts right now:

I don't like soccer.

There. I said it.

Ace benchwarmer Steve Moore dislikes the most popular sport in the world—maybe even the entire universe.

Quick Time-Out about Why I Don't Like Soccer

There are several good reasons, okay? It's not like I'm just cranky.

First of all, unlike the game of basketball, there's not much scoring in soccer. A final score of two to zip is pretty much a blowout.

Scoring is so infrequent that if you look away for even half a second to squash a mosquito that's sucking blood out of your arm, you might miss seeing the only goal of the game.

And soccer players run up and down the field with very few breaks. There are no time-outs, unless you keel over from a broken leg or some other ailment.

And when there's a foul, the ref holds up goofy yellow or red cards. Why not just signal with your hands like in basketball or football?

But the main reason I don't like the game of soccer is that my body has lousy foot-eye coordination. I call it "Foot-Eye Dweeb-Itis."

It's an embarrassing affliction—worse than when you get lice in your hair and then everyone at school finds out about it.

I already told you that I have excellent hand-eye coordination. But if my feet are asked to do anything more than walk, run, or jump, that's when Foot-Eye Dweeb-Itis rears its ugly head.

And in soccer, the feet do most of the work. So someone with foot-eye problems either won't make the team, or, if they do, they'll be sitting on the pine.

I'm pretty sure that Foot-Eye Dweeb-Itis is due to faulty internal communication wiring.

• • •

So soccer doesn't exactly fry my burger. But I made a big mistake by saying so.

Out loud.

Right in front of a best friend.

Who happens to love the game of soccer more than any sport in the entire universe.

It happened at the sports stadium that sits right smack in the middle of my neighborhood.

My best friends and I practically live at Goodfellow Stadium because we all pretty much love everything about sports.

The stadium is really ancient. Archaeologists estimate that it dates back all the way to the early *1980s*.

Old people get all emotional and weepy-eyed whenever they walk through the gates because Goodfellow Stadium has hosted a bunch of "memorable moments." Whatever that means.

The stadium has a rickety domed roof that slides open and closed, so it can host any kind of sport in any conditions, except maybe a category 5 hurricane or a direct hit from an asteroid.

On this particular day, my friends and I got into Goodfellow Stadium for free, as usual, by helping the concessions workers unload boxes from delivery trucks. As a bonus they always give us a treat of our choice.

Joey selected a churro because his tiny, revved-up central nervous system demands a constant supply of sugar.

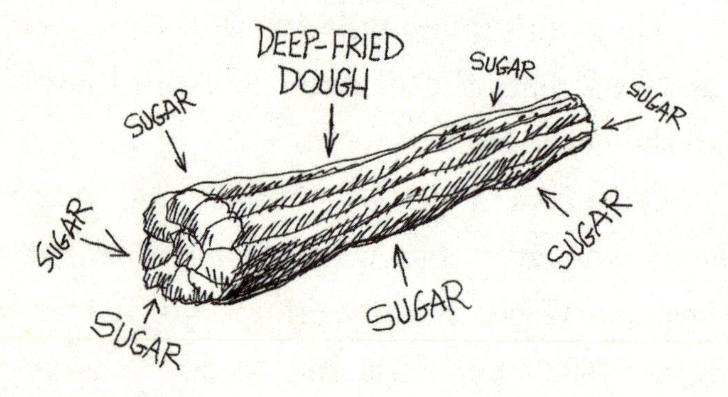

Carlos grabbed a family-size bag of roasted peanuts. He sucks the salt off and then chews up and swallows the peanuts, shell and all.

Becky and I chose the same treat—an Eskimo Pie. It's vanilla ice cream covered in chocolate. In case you don't already know, it's pretty much nature's near-perfect food. (Not a commercial endorsement!)

We were at the stadium to watch our hometown professional soccer team, the Goodfellow Wiseguys, play an exhibition match against FC Barcelona, a hotshot soccer team from Spain.

Our team was getting slaughtered by the Spanish team, one goal to zip.

I wasn't thrilled about watching a soccer match. My friends practically had to drag me to the stadium. But Joey, Carlos, and Becky are soccer fanatics.

Becky was especially excited. She knew all about the FC Barcelona team. She even knew the first and last names and personal backgrounds of every one of their hotshot players.

We were sitting way up in the very top bleachers, right under where the lice-infested pigeons roost.

Our good friend Billionaire Bill was walking around the upper decks of Goodfellow Stadium blasting an air horn to scare the pigeons out of the rafters so that spectators wouldn't need umbrellas to protect their heads. If you know what I mean.

Bill is the stadium's official "pigeon-control officer."

He calls himself a "bleacher bum" because Bill actually lives in a cramped "apartment" beneath the bleachers for free in return for his important pigeon duties.

Bill once was a very successful and respected rocket scientist. Or a star player in the NBA. Maybe an umbrella salesman. I forget.

Anyway, his previous life apparently got way too comfortable, so he decided to shake things up and get out of what he calls his "comfort zone."

Next to my mom and dad, Billionaire Bill is my favorite adult role model in the entire world.

Bill took a break from blasting the air horn at the pigeons and sat down with us.

He usually offers all kinds of wisdom that anyone would be foolish to ignore. But this time Bill looked down on the soccer field and said something that I didn't exactly agree with.

There was less than a minute left in the match between the Wiseguys and the hotshot Spanish guys and a grand total of *one* goal had been scored. What's magic about that?

To me, it was boring to watch. So I expressed my honest opinion about the most popular game in the entire universe.

I didn't say it very loud or anything. It was more like a mumble, but I immediately regretted saying it—especially because I used the h-word.

The Power Structure (Mom and Dad)

practically made me poke my finger with a needle and sign my name in blood on a legal contract promising to never use that word. Ever.

And on top of that, Becky heard me.

Derp!

She turned and stared at me for what felt like three hours, but it was probably only three seconds. Then Becky stood up and, without saying a word, walked down from the bleachers and out of Goodfellow Stadium while the boring soccer match was still in progress.

Billionaire Bill looked at me as if I'd just cut cheese. Then *he* got up and went back to earning his rent by terrorizing lice-infested pigeons with an air horn.

About ten seconds after Becky and Bill left, the Goodfellow Wiseguys scored back-to-back goals in the final seconds and creamed the hotshot soccer team from Spain, two goals to one.

And I'm not even making that up!

Becky tried to avoid me at school the next day.

That's really hard to do at Spiro T. Agnew Middle School because students are packed into a building that is barely big enough to fit everyone. And it smells like melted crayons.

The school was built in the ancient 1970s. I think it might be a historic site like one of those pyramids in Egypt where dead pharaohs are lying around just trying to get some rest for all eternity.

Our school was named after a vice president who resigned from office for being corrupt. I don't know what he did, but it must have been serious. I don't think vice presidents resign just because they get caught chewing gum during a meeting or for speaking without raising their hand.

Anyway, it's hard to avoid running into other students at Spiro. The hallways are very narrow. Everyone migrates between classes like wildebeest with backpacks, but there's not much noise because the hallways are carpeted.

Why? I don't know. You'd have to ask Mother T. She's the school principal who had the loud linoleum ripped out and quiet carpeting installed.

Mother T insists that students whisper—*whisper*—while struggling just to survive during the migration between classes. She is a tiny and frail woman, but Mother T has a mysterious power over students' brains, just like that old geezer in the Star Wars movies.

Becky had dodged me in the carpeted hallway between first and second periods. But the migration pattern between second and third periods put us face-to-face in the hallway.

When we met up, I did that remorseful thing where you lower your eyes and shuffle feet and stick hands in pockets and try to apologize but nothing comes out of your mouth.

Becky is probably the nicest person in the world, with Nature's Near-Perfect Smile, so she wasn't even angry or anything. Mostly she seemed disappointed.

Becky asked if I had ever played soccer.

I did mess around with a soccer ball a few times, but I admitted that I'd never actually played soccer, like in an organized game.

Er . . . I lowered my eyes. Shuffled feet. Stuck hands in my pockets.

Becky squeezed past me and disappeared into the mass migration in the carpeted hallway of Spiro T. Agnew Middle School.

If you want to know the truth, I'd much rather have a best friend be angry with me because then I'd know exactly how to respond. A sincere apology, without wimpy excuses, usually smooths things over.

Disappointment, though, is harder to fix.

When I got home from school, I went to my bedroom and let Fido out of his cage.

I happen to love animals, and I have several pets.

Fido is my pet boa constrictor. He is by far the coolest pet in the entire universe. Fido can grow to ten feet, which is big enough to swallow a French poodle.

And my family just happens to have a French poodle. Frenchy is by far the most demented dog in the entire universe. And I'm not even exaggerating.

Frenchy lives under my bed and only comes out when it's absolutely necessary to "do his business" in the backyard.

Frenchy doesn't do normal dog stuff like playing fetch or vomiting on clean carpets or rolling in the rotting corpses of salmon.

I think he'd actually *like* doing that dog stuff, but Frenchy has never even tried.

He has his little comfort zone under my bed, where he just lies around and thinks about, er, whatever demented poodles think about all day.

I plopped down on my bed to think of a way to make up for opening my big mouth in front of Becky and my friends at the boring soccer match.

I kicked around some ideas . . .

Buy her an Eskimo Pie?

Lame.

Compliment her Nature's Near-Perfect Smile?

Lamer.

Offer to carry her tray in the cafeteria?

Lamest.

I was stumped.

Then Fido wandered under my bed, in a snake sort of way. Frenchy growled and barked and tried to act all threatening because Fido had invaded his precious comfort zone.

Fido blew him off, though, because snakes rarely get intimidated. As a sign of friendship, Fido "kicked" a tennis ball that had been gathering dust under my bed for at least five years.

Snakes have excellent tail-eye coordination.

The ball rolled into the middle of the room, and Frenchy crawled out from under my bed and retrieved the dusty tennis ball just like a normal dog!

Frenchy immediately reverted to his old ways and crawled back under my bed, but Fido had done something no one else in my family had been able to do. The snake had gotten the psychotic poodle out of his comfort zone—even if it was only for a few seconds.

That reminded me of wise advice my grandpa Jim taught me but that, apparently, I had forgotten.

Quick Time-Out about Grandpa Jim

Gramps lives on a sailboat on the island of Maui in Hawaii with Ulupalakua, an African gray parrot who has the vocabulary of a thirty-five-year-old man with a snotty attitude. And I'm not even making that up.

He talks in complete snotty sentences.

(I'm not exactly sure why grandpa doesn't just open the hatch of his sailboat and command his snotty pal to fly off to some other more appropriate living situation.)

I don't see Grandpa Jim very often because he rarely leaves Hawaii. He's sort of a hermit. Gramps has long hair and a beard and overgrown eyebrows that look like caterpillars with lousy personal hygiene.

But he sends me texts practically every day and sometimes he attaches videos of Ulupalakua making snotty comments about current fashion and music trends.

My dad told me that Grandpa Jim is a veteran of a war that happened way back in the days before smartphones were invented.

During one of Grandpa Jim's rare visits to our house, he noticed at dinner that I wasn't eating the broccoli that was being served.

I had never eaten broccoli. My parents had tried to get me to eat it, but I didn't like the way it looked or smelled, so I figured the taste wouldn't exactly fry my burger. They finally gave up.

But Grandpa Jim loves broccoli, so he jabbed me with his elbow and whispered in my ear.

I don't know why, but advice from a grandparent always seems more reasonable than advice from a parent.

So I tried the broccoli. It didn't make me gag or lapse into convulsions, but it didn't exactly fry my burger.

And I was worried that eating broccoli would make my eyebrows grow into caterpillars with lousy personal hygiene.

• • •

I remembered Grandpa Jim's advice after Frenchy briefly crawled out of his comfort zone to fetch the dusty tennis ball.

Don't knock it until you try it.

There was only one thing to do if I was going to save my friendship with Becky O'Callahan.

No! Not that.

I made up my mind to suck it up, break out of my comfort zone, and try out for the Spiro T. Agnew soccer team.

By the time I got to school the next day, I was having second thoughts about playing soccer with my Foot-Eye Dweeb-Itis. I didn't want to embarrass myself in front of the entire world.

But at lunch break, it became clear that I really didn't have a choice.

In the cafeteria, where gossip is like a nasty virus with no vaccine, I sensed that people were talking about me.

I thought someone at school had spilled

the beans about my "I hate soccer" comment.

I went through the food line and got a plate of the "Mighty Plumbers Special," which was just canned tuna dumped into a vat of pinto beans.

Then I walked with my tray toward the C Central table, where Joey, Carlos, Becky, and I usually sit.

I was pretty sure other students in the cafeteria were gossiping about me and how I hate the most popular sport in the universe.

Or maybe not.

Did someone spill the beans? There were three prime suspects: Becky, Joey, or Carlos.

Becky wasn't even sitting at the C Central table anymore because of my "I hate soccer" blunder. But she is too nice to spread gossip.

And Joey speaks too quietly for anyone to hear him, even if he did gossip.

That left Carlos.

But it wasn't Carlos. In fact, no one had spilled the beans.

Yet.

Jimmy Jimerino is Spiro's BJOC—Big Jock on Campus. He and his kiss-up posse of clingy friends stopped at the C Central table. Jimmy pointed at me.

Oh, derp. *Now* the beans were spilled.

Jimmy's kiss-up posse laughed like hyenas. Everyone in the cafeteria stopped scarfing their food. They turned and stared at me.

Now I *really* had no choice. If there was any hope of saving my friendship with Becky and patching up my reputation at school, then I had to follow my grandpa's advice:

"Don't knock it until you try it."

After the final period of classes, I walked into the athletic office to sign up for the varsity soccer team tryouts.

CHAPTER 6

I was too late.

The deadline for signing up had already passed. Tryouts were over and Coach Earwax had posted the final team roster on the wall outside his office.

Those who'd made the cut were the usual hotshot athletes. Jimmy Jimerino, of course, was at the top of the list. He and his posse of clingy friends.

Guys like Skinny Dennis and Vinny

Pascual and Dewey Taylor. They laugh their jocks off at every lame joke that Jimmy tells—even if they've heard him tell the same joke a million times.

Becky O'Callahan's name also was on the list of players who made the team. Becky is a hotshot athlete, but without all the attitude.

I walked into Coach Earwax's office to ask if I could play on the soccer team, even though tryouts were over. He was a little, er, preoccupied.

Coach Earwax has a semi-secret habit. He digs wax out of his ears with car keys. Then he rolls the wax up into a ball and sticks it under his chair like chewed bubble gum. His head is practically a wax factory.

I had to do one of those fake COUGH things that alert a person with a semi-secret habit that someone else is in the room.

Coach quickly ditched a huge wad of earwax under his chair.

I asked him if I could join the varsity team even if it meant that I had to sit on the bench and never play unless the score was a hundred to zip. (Which would never in a billion years happen in the game of soccer.)

I was perfectly fine with sitting on the pine. Like I said, I'm good at it. And I enjoy watching all the stuff that goes on around the game, like Coach digging wax out of his ears with car keys.

Coach Earwax turned me down, though. He said it wouldn't be fair to players who actually tried out for the team, especially the ones who got cut and had to live with the humiliation for a week or two until they got over it.

But Coach Earwax suggested an alternative if I really was serious about playing soccer.

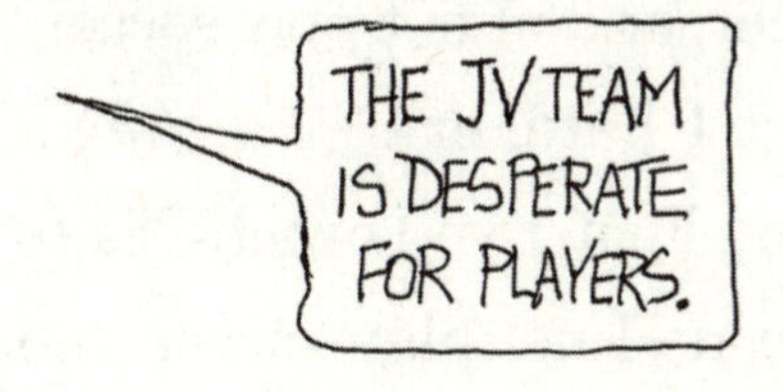

I stood outside the office of the JV soccer coach for a long time. My mind bounced back and forth: Do I play soccer, or do I not play soccer?

Do I play a sport I hate, er . . . *dislike a lot* . . . and reveal my Foot-Eye Dweeb-Itis to the entire world? Or do I not play soccer and lose a good friend with Nature's Near-Perfect Smile.

I walked into the coach's office. Ms. Katinsky was standing at the window and gazing out at the parking lot. She was reciting dialogue from what I think is a famous play. Or maybe a novel. Animated movie? I'm not sure.

Anyway, it was something about a dumb cat that foolishly climbed onto a roof in the middle of summer.

Ms. Katinsky coaches the JV soccer team and a couple of other sports, but her main job at Spiro is teaching theater.

You probably already know this, but teachers don't exactly rake in the cash. So coaching is a side job that Ms. Katinsky works to earn a few extra bucks for stuff like food and shelter.

She goes by "Ms. Katinsky" in theater class, but in sports the players call her "Coach K" because it's a strict rule in every sport that a coach has a nickname.

I didn't need to do one of those fake COUGH things to alert Coach K that I was in the room. Catching someone who is alone and reciting dialogue about a foolish cat isn't as awkward as walking in on a coach who digs wax out of his ears with car keys.

I got down to business and sort of begged Coach K. to let me play on the JV soccer team.

I told her that I *totally forgot* about tryouts for the varsity team, which was a minor fib.

Then I explained how my body needs physical activity in order for my brain to comprehend mathematics, which was a bigger fib that I made up on the spot.

And then I told her that I love the game of soccer *more than any sport in the universe,* which was a gigantic whopper.

I was just about to tell Coach K that I'd be willing to sit on the bench, even if the score was an unlikely blowout of a hundred to zip, but she interrupted my pathetic groveling.

Before I went to my first practice as a member of the Spiro T. Agnew junior varsity team, I needed to buy some soccer gear.

I have lots of football, basketball, and baseball gear. I even have golf clubs and a hockey stick and running shoes. But I didn't have a single piece of soccer stuff.

In my family, the Power Structure controls pretty much everything, but Dad is the go-to person whenever I need money to buy any kind of sports gear.

Dad was a hotshot athlete who blew out both of his knees playing sports in college. He missed out on raking in billions in cash playing professional sports. And I'm not even exaggerating.

He shook off the disappointment, though, and now he's a hotshot salesman for a company that makes medical gizmos that repair blown-out knees.

I told Dad that I was going to play soccer for my school.

Next stop, O'Callahan's Sporting Goods.

When I got there, Joey and Carlos were waiting for me. They knew what I was up to.

This happens a lot. Why? Because Joey is

psychic. And I'm not even making that up.

One time, Joey predicted that the Mighty Plumbers mascot would kick Carlos right in the shin, one of the most sensitive bones in the entire body. *And two minutes later, it happened!*

Joey got a psychic message earlier in the day and told Carlos that I was going to play soccer for the JV team and that I had hit up my dad for a chunk of his hard-earned wages to buy gear.

Like I said, Joey and Carlos love soccer. But they both had missed tryouts for the varsity team due to extenuating circumstances.

Joey is the middle child in a big family, so he not only gets lost in the chaos, but he also gets stuck doing unpleasant chores. And that's what happened on the day of soccer tryouts.

Meanwhile, Carlos missed the tryouts because he assumed that Coach Earwax already knew he was a hotshot soccer player who automatically would be notified of the date and time of varsity tryouts.

That didn't happen, for obvious reasons.

So Joey and Carlos decided to play for the JV team, especially when Joey predicted that I was going to be on the team, too. They went to O'Callahan's Sporting Goods to get some gear of their own.

Joey needed shin guards because he couldn't use hand-me-downs. His older siblings had already gone through their "growth spurt," so their shin guards didn't fit Joey. Not even close.

Carlos wasn't there to buy soccer gear, though. He wanted a hacky sack. Why? I don't know. You'd have to ask Carlos.

We walked into O'Callahan's Sporting Goods and Becky was working at the checkout counter. Her grandfather owns the store, so Becky pretty much has a job for life unless she decides to become a brain surgeon or a ventriloquist.

I was about to approach Becky and tell her that I had decided to play soccer for the Spiro JV team so that she wouldn't think I was a heartless soccer hater.

Unfortunately, hotshot athlete Jimmy Jimerino was hanging out at the counter. (Becky used to be Jimmy's girlfriend until she decided that the relationship didn't exactly fry her burger.)

Jimmy apparently was groveling to win her back. He was leaning on the counter, acting all cool in a game-worn NFL jersey that may or may not have been signed by the actual Hall of Fame quarterback who wore it.

(I have a hobby of collecting and selling sports memorabilia. I'd sold that game-worn NFL jersey to Jimmy a few months earlier for about four times what it was actually worth.)

I wasn't in the mood to apologize to Becky right in front of Jimmy, so I snuck past them and went to pick out my soccer gear.

It took Joey about five seconds to grab his tiny shin guards and get to the checkout counter.

Carlos took *way* longer to find the perfect hacky sack.

In case you don't know, hacky sack is a game played with a tennis ball–size bag filled with sand or beads.

Players stand in a circle and kick the bag around with their feet until they quit out of boredom and wander off to find a game that's more fun to play.

After squeezing about a thousand different hacky sacks, Carlos finally chose a bag with just the right amount of sand or beads.

Then he borrowed some of my dad's hard-earned wages to make the purchase because he forgot to bring his wallet, which happens a lot.

Why did I lend Carlos money to buy a hacky sack? I don't know. You'd have to ask . . . er . . . me.

Anyway, I didn't know much about soccer gear, so I winged it and grabbed stuff that I thought might be useful.

I picked out a pair of shorts and a jersey and socks and shin guards. Then I chose a pair of cleats from a wall display of shoes for every game in the universe except hacky sack.

The shoes I picked looked like maybe they would help my feet communicate with my eyes.

I set my gear up on the checkout counter. Becky acted friendly, but it was awkward. It was more like the "friendly" she showed every other O'Callahan's customer.

Our friendship, if we still had one, was

not the same as it was before I trash-talked the most popular game in the universe. So I told Becky that I was going to play soccer for Spiro, hoping that would smooth things over.

Jimmy Jimerino, of course, had to point out that the Spiro varsity roster already was set in stone.

I kept my mouth shut.

Becky rang up the shorts and jersey and socks and shin guards, but not the shoes. She handed them back to me.

Derp!

Jimmy snickered while I swapped the rugby shoes for actual soccer shoes. Then I handed over the last of my dad's hard-earned wages and left O'Callahan's Sporting Goods without saying another word to Becky or Jimmy.

The mission to save my friendship with Becky—and my reputation at school—had begun.

The next step was a big one: the first day of soccer practice, where I would try to overcome my Foot-Eye Dweeb-Itis.

Coach K started practice like every other coach in the entire world. Sort of.

Because she teaches theater, Coach K did it in a dramatic way. Instead of blowing a wimpy whistle, she carried a tuba onto the soccer field and blasted a deep note that sounded like a water buffalo with stomach gas.

The tuba blast startled one of the players so badly, he ran off the field and never came back.

We started practice with conditioning drills that didn't require that my feet communicate properly with my eyes.

It was all push-ups, sit-ups, and laps around the field. Everyone cruised through it without any problem. Except cranky Carlos.

Then Coach K brought out the soccer balls for a fundamentals drill. She had each of us pair off with another teammate and stand ten feet apart.

I ended up with Liz Casey, a popular girl who is the student body president. Liz has a habit of speaking in sentences that all end in question marks.

No periods. No exclamation marks. Only question marks.

I'm pretty sure that's why Liz was doing so well in school politics because she never actually made a campaign promise that ended with a period.

After everyone paired off for the fundamentals drill, Coach K told us to kick the soccer ball back and forth.

There was no question that Liz's feet knew how to communicate with her eyes.

She did that thing where the ball is on the ground and you spin it up onto the toe of your shoe, fling it up in the air, and then kick the ball to another player.

Liz spun it, flung it, and kicked the ball over to me. I was supposed to stop the ball with my foot, control it, then kick it back to Liz.

It didn't go well.

Liz tried to be nice and took the blame.

"Sorry? That was totally my fault?"

I kicked the ball back to Liz, but it veered

off. Every time she kicked it to me, I couldn't stop and control the ball. And every time I kicked the ball back to Liz, it would sail off in a wrong direction.

Meanwhile, my hands were weak and useless.

They played no role in the soccer drill. They just sort of dangled by my side while my feet and eyes suffered a total communication breakdown.

At one point, Coach K stopped by to see how Liz and I were doing. After observing a few of my botched kicks, she taught me a fundamental that most soccer players learn when they are about two years old.

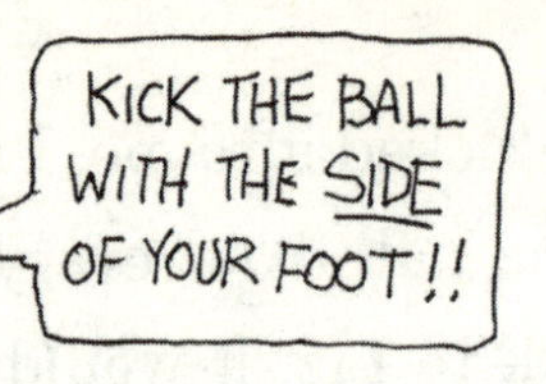

I have always kicked with the *toe* of my foot. I had never kicked *anything* with the side of my foot. Not a football or a beach ball or a pile of leaves—nothing!

I gave it a try, but by then the wiring between my feet and eyes was completely bumfuzzled.

The soccer drill went on for way too long, in my opinion.

Coach K finally blasted her tuba. It was

time for a scrimmage.

Because one of the players had been frightened earlier by the tuba blast and ran off never to be seen again, we only had twelve players, so Coach K divided us into two practice squads with six players each.

In regulation soccer, each team has eleven players on the field and at least three or four substitutes on the bench.

So why did we have so few players?

Jessica Whitehead, the school genius, told me that some of Spiro's best soccer players chose to play for elite club teams that aren't associated with a school.

The clubs cost parents a huge chunk of their hard-earned wages, but apparently they give hotshot soccer players a better chance for a college scholarship and a career in the pros, where they will rake in billions in cash.

Spiro didn't have enough players for separate boys and girls soccer teams. So we had varsity and JV teams that were coed.

I was on one scrimmage team with Joey and four others, including Liz Casey, who apparently had taken a liking to Joey.

Carlos was on the other team with Jessica Whitehead. Carlos and Jessica once were sort of "a thing." But that only lasted about a week.

Stephanie Jennison also was on Carlos's squad. She was by far the best player on the Spiro JV soccer team.

Stephanie missed varsity tryouts because her family had just moved to town.

She was good enough to have deserted Spiro to play for an elite soccer club, but Stephanie wanted to be true to her new school. (Or maybe her parents didn't want to fork over a huge chunk of their hard-earned wages to pay for an elite club.)

Carlos was chosen to kick off from midfield to start the scrimmage.

Carlos had told Coach K that he was a hotshot player who should play center midfielder—pretty much the most important offensive position in the game of soccer.

Carlos, of course, had told Coach K a gigantic whopper.

Instead of doing the smart thing and tapping the ball to a teammate, self-proclaimed hotshot Carlos started the scrimmage by kicking the soccer ball as hard as he could downfield.

It was an impressive kick, but it curved out of bounds and into the faculty parking lot, where it ricocheted among the economy cars and set off about a dozen alarms.

We began the scrimmage.

Carlos lumbered around the field, grumbling about multiple "fouls," and he pretty much proved to Coach K that he was not even close to being a decent center midfielder.

Joey was awesome. He was so quick, the other players couldn't even see him steal the ball right from under their legs.

Coach K wrote a top-secret note in her clipboard about Joey's quick-as-a-flea abilities.

Eleven of the twelve players in the scrimmage kicked the ball up and down the field. Meanwhile, the twelfth player—that would be me—avoided the ball.

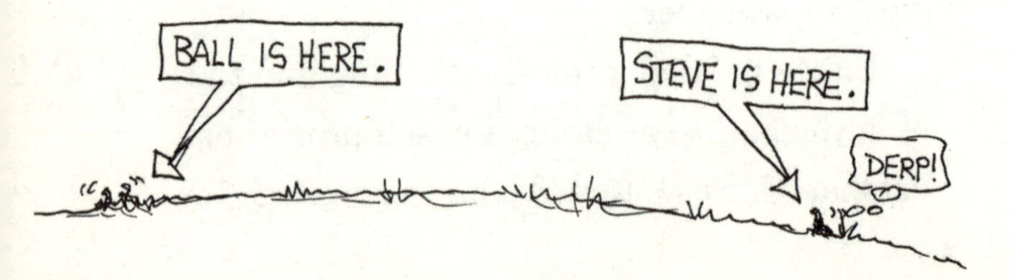

I didn't want to put my Foot-Eye Dweeb-Itis on display.

Coach K finally stopped the scrimmage and, right in front of the other players, asked me if I was afraid of the soccer ball.

Ouch!

That brought back bad memories of my first season on the Spiro T. Agnew baseball team when I had Bean-O-Phobia, a morbid fear of getting hit by a pitch.

But I defeated that phobia long ago.

I wasn't afraid of the soccer ball. I was afraid of what my clueless feet would *do* with the soccer ball. So I tried to bluff.

To show that I wasn't afraid, I foolishly went after the ball whenever it came anywhere near me. Here is a short summary of how that worked out:

Coach K ended practice and called us into a tight huddle. It was a little too tight for Joey.

Coach handed out the schedule for the soccer season. We had to practice every day after school for a week before we started preseason games.

And the first JV and varsity preseason games on our schedule were every player's dream: A bus trip. To an out-of-town soccer tournament. For an entire *weekend*!

I was excited about having fun on a bus trip to another town and hanging out in a hotel and playing a few games. It offers all kinds of opportunity for shenanigans.

But I also was worried. Not only would my Foot-Eye-Dweeb-Itis be on display, but I once had a bad experience on a bus trip to an out-of-town tournament.

Quick Time-Out about That Bus Trip

It was in first grade. I traveled to a Teeny-Weeny Hoops tournament in a town that was a four-hour bus ride away.

The road trip was a blast for the first three hours. We guzzled Gatorade and stuffed our faces with candy and sunflower seeds and pulled all kinds of shenanigans that drove the coaches and chaperones right out of their skulls.

But all the Teeny-Weeny basketball players fell silent during the final hour.

The bus didn't have a restroom. And the driver was stubborn and cranky. He refused to stop for a break.

That's a recipe for disaster when there are a bunch of first graders with teeny-weeny bladders on board who have been guzzling Gatorade for three hours.

I averted disaster—barely—by closing my eyes, crossing my legs, and clenching my teeth for the final hour. But others on the bus couldn't control their faucet. If you know what I mean.

Including Carlos. To this day, he swears the bus hit a bump in the road, which knocked a bottle of lemon Gatorade onto his lap.

When we finally pulled up to the hotel, there was a mad rush of kids with full bladders pushing and shoving to get out the bus door and into a restroom.

I got trampled in the stampede. There was no way I could make it into the hotel and wait in a long line for the restroom. So I took a detour.

I didn't end up with "lemon Gatorade" on my pants like Carlos and the others. But since then I have avoided out-of-town trips on a bus with no restroom and a driver who is stubborn and cranky.

• • •

Coach K dismissed the JV team just as the varsity soccer squad arrived for their practice.

Jimmy Jimerino and his kiss-up posse trotted onto the field like God's gift to soccer. They loitered at midfield and laughed like hyenas at Jimmy's worn-out jokes.

Then the best player on the varsity soccer team ran onto the field and started warming up.

It was Becky.

We made eye contact and I tried to smile, but my mouth got stuck.

I gathered up an armload of gear to help out Coach K and I tried to slink away. But Jimmy Jimerino spotted me.

He shouted across the field loud enough for everyone in the town of Goodfellow to hear.

Jimmy's posse of kiss-ups laughed their hotshot shorts off.

That night at home I gave the parental permission sheet for the out-of-town soccer trip to the Moore family Power Structure.

Dad, of course, signed immediately. He didn't even read the details. All he knew was that his son would be playing a sport.

Mom, however, examined the permission sheet as if it was a legal contract to sell our house and all of our worldly possessions.

My mom is a turbo-hyper-worrywart, so she sees anything having to do with sports as a possible cause of bodily injury.

And she is a big fan of helmets. Mom is 100 percent certain that a helmet will protect me from any kind of harm in life—like a wild pitch or a direct hit from an asteroid.

Mom knew even less about the game of soccer than I did.

Derp!

Dad had to explain to Mom that there are no helmets in soccer because players hardly ever get their faces smashed into the grass like in football.

On the day of our trip, everyone going to the weekend soccer tournament got to leave school in the middle of their final period. In my case, that was perfect timing.

The varsity and JV teams filed onto the bus. As we boarded, Miss Ekolie, the cafeteria manager, handed out our snack bags. We were all excited until we looked inside the bag.

Kale!

We all knew that Mother T had to be responsible for *that* dirty trick.

On school trips, my friends and I always try to get seats in the very back of the bus, where we can get away with all kinds of shenanigans.

It never works out that way.

Jimmy Jimerino and his kiss-up posse always push and shove their way past everyone and call dibs on all of the excellent shenanigan seats at the back of the bus.

My friends and I got stuck in the front of the bus in seats next to the JV and varsity coaches.

Becky O'Callahan was the last player to board the bus. She doesn't care all that much where she sits. But she didn't get stuck sitting up front next to the coaches because Ricky Schnauzer had saved her a seat next to him.

Ricky Schnauzer!

This was the same guy who got cut from the Spiro baseball team and then hid in a toilet stall because of the shame. Then he decided that playing football for Spiro didn't exactly fry his burger, so he quit and volunteered as team equipment manager.

But, apparently, Ricky does not suffer from Foot-Eye Dweeb-Itis because he had made the cut for the Spiro varsity soccer team.

Becky walked by me without smiling Nature's Near-Perfect Smile or even saying hello.

After she passed by, I looked back.

Ricky got up and stood in the aisle. He was wearing a neatly pressed shirt, sport coat, and tie. He motioned for Becky to take the prime window seat.

Wow.

And just when I thought things couldn't get any worse, the bus driver got on board. And he looked familiar.

Very familiar.

He was the same stubborn and cranky

driver who refused to stop during my Teeny-Weeny basketball trip!

The driver sat down behind the wheel and looked up into the rearview mirror. He stared back at me with an evil, "I'm not gonna stop for a break" grin on his face.

I think he might have even recognized me from first grade.

And I'm not even making that up!

I turned and looked in the back of the bus.

There was no restroom.

Just Jimmy Jimerino and his kiss-up posse sprawled out in the rear seats chugging bottles of Gatorade.

I had a bottle, too, but I had only taken

one or two or maybe six gulps.

I quickly stashed it in my carry-on bag. Then I warned Joey and Carlos about the stubborn and cranky driver from Teeny-Weeny Hoops and our bus with no restroom.

Joey didn't seem too concerned because, for a tiny guy, he has a gigantic bladder.

But Carlos reacted as if he might pass out. I looked on the floor under his seat. There were three—*three*—empty Gatorade bottles. And we hadn't even left the parking lot!

I thought about alerting the coaches so they could make an emergency announcement in case anyone wanted to sprint to the restroom one more time before we left, but it was too late.

The stubborn and cranky driver shut the doors. We were trapped.

Our bus with no restroom rolled out of the Spiro T. Agnew parking lot on a four-hour road trip with no possibility of a rest break.

I was sitting in the front of the bus next to the coaches with no possibility of shenanigans. So I slunk down in my seat and tried to make the time pass quickly.

I did the usual road-trip stuff.

I listened to music. I stared out the window at billboards and cattle in pastures slurping up grass and a big rig that had overturned and dumped two tons of broccoli—*broccoli*—onto the side of the highway.

I shifted in my seat about a million times. And I tried to sleep, but the rigid bus seat kept my neck bent at a painful angle.

Meanwhile, the other players on the bus partied in shenanigans for three hours.

Then they all fell silent.

I felt discomfort in my bladder, but it wasn't like a major flood was imminent because I had completely cut off my intake of liquids.

But others on the bus weren't doing so well.

It was the beginning of an epic event that later became known in Spiro T. Agnew folklore as the Great Gatorade Bladder Massacre.

Jimmy Jimerino and his kiss-up posse

seemed to be especially stressed. There were dozens of empty Gatorade bottles scattered on the floor under their seats.

Bladders from the back of the bus to the front were maxed out. Bulging. But the stubborn, cranky, and apparently evil bus driver kept rolling down the highway.

Occasionally, he'd look up in the rearview mirror and gaze back upon all the weak and useless passengers squirming in their seats.

He had his creepy, "I'm not gonna stop for a break" grin on his face.

Carlos was miserable. He was bent over in his seat with legs double-crossed. If it was humanly possible, I think Carlos would have triple-crossed his legs.

Meanwhile, tiny Joey and his big bladder were doing just fine.

We arrived in the town of Laurensville, where the Laurensville Invitational Soccer Tournament was being held. That's why they call it the Laurensville . . . Oh, never mind.

The instant the bus stopped and the evil bus driver opened the doors, there was a chaotic dash of passengers out of the bus and into the hotel restrooms.

Jimmy Jimerino charged up the aisle to the front door and knocked over everyone in his path—even members of his kiss-up posse.

Dewey Taylor actually tried to clear a path like a loyal fullback so Jimmy could get out of the bus and into the hotel restroom. But Jimmy plowed right over Dewey just like the others.

Players screamed and whimpered. Dewey tripped on a curb and fell on his face, chipping a front tooth. And a grown woman was so frightened by the stampede that she fainted!

Meanwhile, I had to shake Joey by the shoulders to wake him up—otherwise he would have slept in the bus through the entire weekend soccer tournament.

All through the climax of the Great Gatorade Bladder Massacre, the stubborn and cranky bus driver sat in his seat and watched it unfold with a creepy, "I didn't stop once" grin on his face.

All the out-of-town soccer teams were staying at the Laurensville Garden Hotel. It was a decent place, with no obvious signs of bedbugs or decay, but there was no actual garden that I could see. Just a few wimpy flower beds.

The first order of business was room assignments, which in most cases were decided days in advance because everyone bunked with their closest friends.

Everyone except Ricky Schnauzer. Ricky reserved a room for himself, probably so that he had enough space for his neatly pressed wardrobe.

Joey, Carlos, and I shared a room, of course. The Three Benchkateers always stick together.

There were only two beds in our room, so we did rock, paper, scissors to decide who would get stuck sleeping on the lumpy couch. It came down to me and Carlos.

After Carlos calmed down and tossed his stuff on the couch, we explored the hotel.

It was crawling with soccer players from the top floor to the bottom floor and everywhere in between—in the elevators and the hallways and the lobby and the pool and the Jacuzzi and the wimpy flower beds.

And wherever we wandered, players from other schools were gossiping about a mysterious player on the Nike Preparatory Academy team who supposedly was the best soccer player his age in the entire universe.

(That last one was my favorite.)

Few people outside of Nike Prep knew the mysterious player's real name, but his nickname was Thunderfoot.

I met him early the next morning at the Laurensville Garden Hotel's delicious buffet breakfast. (Not a commercial endorsement!)

I remembered Thunderfoot from football season.

He was the kicker for Nike Prep who once booted a football *barefoot* out of Spiro's stadium, over the parking lot and onto Seventh Avenue. It landed on the roof of a police cruiser a block away and almost created a SWAT incident.

And I'm not even making that up.

At breakfast, Thunderfoot was standing barefoot in line ahead of me waiting to get waffles, even though his plate already was piled high with scrambled eggs, bacon, sausage, biscuits, and hash browns.

It was early in the morning when ordinary people would be grumpy and puffy-eyed and their breath would smell like a sock that was worn way too many days in a row.

But Thunderfoot is no ordinary person. His eyes were bright and shiny. He turned around and gave me a big smile.

And his breath was fresh and minty.

Quick Time-Out about Thunderfoot

I'm at least 72 percent sure that what I was told about Thunderfoot is the absolute truth.

Joey's former next-door neighbor has a cousin whose best friend's stepsister's friend attends Nike Preparatory Academy.

And she says Thunderfoot is a foreign exchange student from Brazil.

He was just a snot-nosed kid in a public school in the city of São Paulo, but Thunderfoot was pretty much a martial-arts soccer wizard with gravity defying moves who had the power to kick a ball barefoot right through the trunk of a tree!

So word of Thunderfoot leaked out, and schools from around the world sent recruiters to São Paulo with offers of full-ride scholarships and soccer glory.

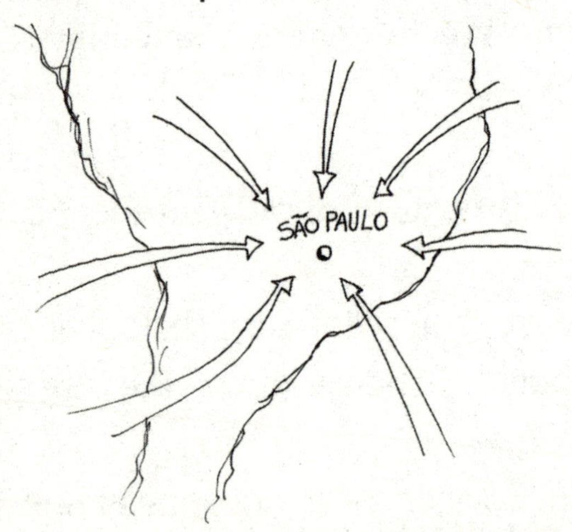

Thunderfoot's parents chose Nike Preparatory Academy because the school put academics first and sports second. But not just soccer. They wanted him to play more than one sport.

And that's the 72 percent absolute truth about Thunderfoot.

• • •

Later that day, I watched Thunderfoot display his barefoot martial-arts soccer skills.

The Spiro JV team wasn't scheduled to play until the afternoon, so my friends and I—and practically every other person who was not involved in a game—watched the first-round match between the Nike Prep Platypuses and the Chaney Middle School Werewolves.

Chaney has a reputation as a frightening school. Their players are really mean and kind of hairy. And the meanest, hairiest Werewolves player is nicknamed "Beast."

He is gigantic and muscular. And smelly. Beast is the dominant player in every sport at Chaney. Except golf.

Nike Prep, meanwhile, is an odd little school that excels in academics. And the Platypuses teams are disciplined and guided by a single motto: "Think positive!"

The Werewolves were favored to maul the competition and pretty much cruise right into the tournament championship.

But they weren't expecting Thunderfoot.

In the first ten seconds of the match, Thunderfoot scored three times.

He spun around Beast and scored. He darted under Beast and scored. He kicked the ball into the air and leaped up over Beast's head.

And then, in midair, he kicked the ball into the goal—all the way from *midfield*!

I lost count, but Nike Prep beat Chaney by probably a hundred to zip.

Beast was not happy.

The legend of Thunderfoot kicked into high gear.

Meanwhile, my struggles with Foot-Eye Dweeb-Itis kicked into higher gear.

The Spiro JV team played in the first round against the tournament hosts—Laurensville Middle School, "Home of the Fighting Pinecones."

Coach K picked Joey to play center forward because he's quick as a flea and low to the ground, which gives him maximum ball control.

Carlos still insisted that *he* should play center forward, but he ended up sitting on the bench as our team's only substitute. Carlos was not happy.

Coach K. put me in at defender on the left side. She probably hoped that my Foot-Eye Dweeb-Itis wouldn't do too much damage in that position.

Wrongity, wrong, wrong.

I think the Fighting Pinecones noticed me during warm-ups and detected a slight defect in my ability.

A Pinecones player immediately dribbled the ball my way. I moved in to stop him and steal the ball, but while trying to decide between "kicking and running," my feet got tangled up and I fell flat on my face. The Pinecones player dribbled around me and scored.

Fighting Pinecones one, Mighty Plumbers zip.

Every time the Pinecones attacked the left side, my feet would go all dweeb. I could not stop the ball or control the ball or kick the ball.

Good old Joey kept us in the game.

His low center of gravity and flea-like quickness allowed him to dart in and snatch the ball away from the Pinecones. Then he'd streak downfield faster than the human eye can see.

But every time, after Joey scored, I failed to stop a Nike Prep advance. Either my feet would ignore directions from my eyes and I'd trip and stumble, or my hands would ignore a major rule in the game of soccer.

You know the rule. The one about not catching or even touching the ball with your hands or arms. Big, drool-y *duh*.

Three times—*three times*—I instinctively reached out and grabbed the ball as if I was playing basketball, football, or baseball.

After each of my stupid mistakes, Nike Prep was awarded a free kick. And two of those kicks resulted in goals.

The score was tied at the halftime break, three goals to three. And all of the Pinecones' goals were scored because of my Foot-Eye Dweeb-Itis or my soccer rules brain wreck.

We had a ten-minute break. Coach K gave the team an eight-minute pep talk. Then she spent the final two minutes talking to me while the rest of the team sucked on orange slices because it's a strict rule in soccer that players suck on orange slices during the half-time break.

Coach K sat down next to me and wrapped her arm around my shoulder. Usually, that's a sure sign that you're about to get yanked from the game.

I was prepared to resume my usual position on the pine, but I didn't get benched.

I got relocated.

Coach K compared my situation to what sometimes happens in theater or the movies.

"You were cast in the wrong role."

I suffered from Foot-Eye Dweeb-Itis, but Coach K had noticed that I have good hand-eye coordination. Like when I accidentally grabbed the soccer ball like a loose basket-ball.

So Coach K moved me to the goalkeeper position, where grabbing the ball with your hands is pretty much the most important job. That made me and my bored hands very happy.

Liz Casey, who was playing goalkeeper, moved to my defender position. That made Liz happy. *Very* happy.

In the second half of the match, I hunkered down, knees bent, in front of the goal. I flexed my wrists and fingers. I felt more comfortable. And my feet and eyes reestablished communication.

My hands were free to grab the ball and my feet were free to move without having to stop, control, or kick the soccer ball.

Coach K. even gave me a pair of gloves to improve my grip and help soften the sting when I deflected a kick on goal.

I did feel some pressure, though, because I am an ace benchwarmer, but not a hotshot athlete. And goalkeeper is even more important than center midfielder because—big, drooly *duh*—if there is no goalkeeper, there is a big problem.

The first minutes of the second half, I stopped a couple of weak and useless kicks on goal, but I was starting to have fun—and I wasn't even bored.

Our team no longer had a "weak link" (er, me) to attack, so the Pinecones were having a hard time moving the ball close to the goal.

Meanwhile, Joey did his quick-as-a-flea thing.

We didn't score, but all the action was on the Pinecones' end of the field. And I was feeling confident. Maybe a little too confident.

Joey actually predicted what was going to happen next, although none of us could hear exactly what he said because Joey is really soft-spoken.

About ten seconds later, while the ball was in play on the far end of the field, I got distracted by a rustling noise behind the goal.

A skunk had wandered out of nearby bushes.

Remember when I told you that I love animals? (If you already forgot, that would be really pathetic because it wasn't very many pages ago.)

Well, I love animals but not *all* animals.

Skunks are near the top of the list of

animals that don't exactly fry my burger—right below deathstalker scorpions, pretty much the deadliest scorpion in the entire world.

If you know about skunks and their stanky "natural defense system," then I'm pretty sure I don't need to explain why they rank so high.

My dad taught me on camping trips to *never* challenge a skunk because they always win. So I backed off. WAY off . . .

. . . just as the Pinecones goalkeeper booted the ball from the far end of the field, right over Joey and Liz and Stephanie and every other Mighty Plumbers player.

The ball landed fifteen yards in front of our goal and rolled right into the back of the net.

Fighting Pinecones four, Mighty Plumbers three.

That was bad. But it got worse.

The ball startled the skunk, and it whipped its rear end around and blasted the soccer ball with its stanky natural defense system.

Unfortunately, I was standing within the blast zone.

Oh. My. Derp.

I was covered in stench. Hair. Face. Arms. Legs. Shorts. Jersey. Socks. Shoes.

The smell was so bad that I had to fight the dreaded "gag reflex"—that thing where it feels like you're going to blow chunks, but all you do is gag air and bleat like a goat.

I didn't run. I didn't roll on the ground. I didn't jump up and down like a lunatic. I just stood in front of the goal, frozen, as if the skunk spray had some kind of paralyzing effect.

Coach K and the referee ran toward the goal to see if I was injured or had been frozen by an alien's laser or something, but they both slammed on the breaks as soon as they caught a whiff of the skunk's stanky natural defense system.

I told them a gigantic whopper.

So the ref blew the whistle to continue the game.

The skunk attack had a strange effect on

the outcome of the game.

The Pinecones players didn't want to go anywhere near me and my stank, so they didn't score again for the remainder of the game. Meanwhile, my Mighty Plumbers teammates were so weirded out by the unprovoked skunk attack that they lost focus and also failed to score.

The Fighting Pinecones won the high-scoring match, four goals to three.

After the game, I wasn't exactly welcomed into the traditional lineup where players from both teams file past each other and act all friendly and slap hands and say "good game" even if they don't mean it.

When the Mighty Plumbers JV team lost the match against the Fighting Pinecones, we entered the "consolation bracket." Or, as Jimmy Jimerino called it, the "losers' bracket."

That's where teams go that have zero hope of winning the tournament championship.

We had another game to play. If we won, we'd play a third game to decide the champion of the consolation/losers' bracket. If we lost, we were done.

There were a few hours until our next match, so we all watched the Mighty Plumbers varsity team in their first-round match against Simplot Middle School, "Home of the Blazing Spuds."

There was a big crowd watching the match because the Spiro varsity team was favored to reach the tournament final. The sidelines were lined with players from other teams, coaches, passersby, maybe a few international spies. And, of course, the players' parents.

You probably already know this, but there is a strict social structure for spectators at matches. And soccer parent spectators pretty much rule the sidelines.

Quick Time-Out about Soccer Parents

Here's what I have been told by fairly reliable soccer sources:

There are three types of soccer parents—the Hunky-Dories, the Howlers, and the Buttinskies.

(Maybe four types if you count the No-Shows—parents who would rather eat an entire bowl of live maggots than watch a single soccer match.)

The Hunky-Dories are passive parents. They politely clap and cheer, even for the other team.

They sit placidly in their folding chairs in blazing hot or bitterly cold weather. Hunky-Dories believe that soccer is a fun game that will teach their kids the value of teamwork.

The Howlers are aggressive parents who rush in and plant their folding chairs in the prime spots on the sideline at midfield.

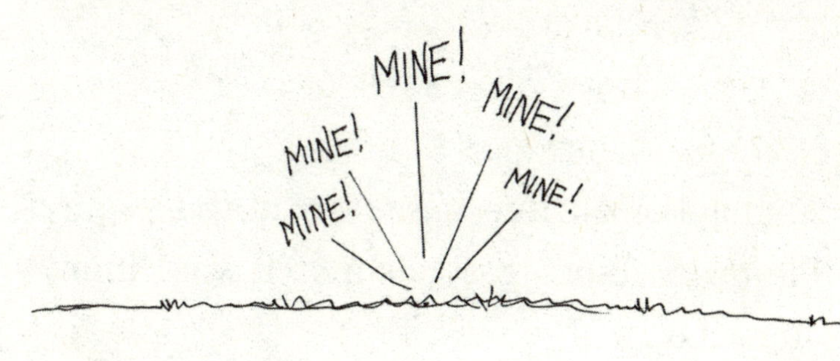

Then they scream their lungs out and criticize referees, coaches, players, Hunky-Dories-pretty much anyone who irritates them.

The Buttinskies are the worst spectators. They are control-freak parents who don't even bother to bring folding chairs to the soccer match because they never sit down. Instead, they roam up and down the sideline and yell instructions to players—especially their own kids.

• • •

Among the sideline spectators at the Mighty Plumbers–Blazing Spuds match was Jimmy Jimerino's dad.

He had made the four-hour drive to the Laurensville tournament, without stopping for a restroom break, to watch his hotshot son dominate the other weak and useless soccer players.

Jimmy could have bolted from Spiro to play for an elite soccer club team, but his dad wanted him to play for a team where Jimmy would be the dominant player.

I watched the Spuds-Plumbers match on

a hill overlooking the end of the soccer field. Joey and Carlos were trying to be all cool and loyal like Benchkateers, but they wisely chose to sit at a safe distance.

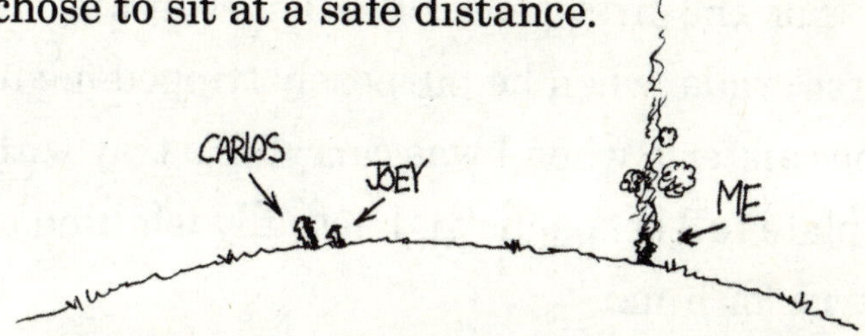

There was no way to get my clothing de-skunked and I didn't have spare gear, so I was surrounded by an invisible cloud of stank.

I had a good view of the game and everything that was happening on the sidelines. It was obvious right away that Mr. Jimerino was a combination of *two* soccer parent types.

He was a Howler *and* a Buttinsky.

Mr. Jimerino brought a folding chair that he firmly planted on the sideline right at the prime midfield mark. But he never even sat in the chair.

Jimmy's dad roamed the sideline and screamed his lungs out and criticized anyone who irritated him. *And* he yelled instructions to the Spiro players as if he was the coach.

Mr. Jimerino was especially hard on his son.

For the first time since I met Jimmy in first grade, when he purposely tripped me in the cafeteria when I was carrying a tray with a plate full of spaghetti, I actually felt kind of sorry for him.

Every time Jimmy got the ball, or was anywhere *near* the ball, his dad would shout at him.

I was beginning to understand why Jimmy Jimerino had become a hotshot BJOC who rules over a posse of kiss-ups at Spiro T. Agnew Middle School.

In the first half of the match, the Mighty Plumbers jumped out to a huge lead over the Blazing Spuds, one goal to zip.

I knew Jimmy Jimerino and his posse of kiss-ups were great soccer players. And I knew Becky O'Callahan was a great soccer player. But I was surprised that Ricky Schnauzer—*Ricky Schnauzer*—was a great soccer player.

On the bus ride to the tournament, Ricky

wore a neatly pressed shirt, sport coat, and tie. And he saved a seat for Becky!

He didn't look like a hotshot soccer player, but I guess you should never judge a book by its cover, as Billionaire Bill always says, because it turned out that Ricky actually had skills as a goalkeeper.

In the match against the Blazing Spuds, Ricky stopped every shot on goal. And I'm not even making that up.

Becky, meanwhile, was scoring goals practically every time she got a foot on the ball. That did not make Jimmy Jimerino happy—or his Howler-Buttinsky dad—because Jimmy considers himself the "go-to guy" in every sport.

But Jimmy had something else on his mind.

Thunderfoot.

The legendary player from Brazil was on the sideline watching the game between the Mighty Plumbers and the Blazing Spuds. He probably showed up to scout the two teams in case his Nike Prep team had to play one of them in the championship game.

When the ball rolled out of bounds in front of Thunderfoot, he picked it up and handed it to a Spiro player—the girl with Nature's Near-Perfect Smile.

I think Becky and Thunderfoot made eye contact for a little too long, though, because Jimmy ran over to the sideline and grabbed the ball out of her hands.

Jimmy tossed the ball back inbounds. Then he turned to Thunderfoot and gave him the major stink eye. But Thunderfoot just smiled.

"Good day, sunshine!"

The Mighty Plumbers varsity team slaughtered the Blazing Spuds, two goals to zip, and moved on to the next round just as everyone expected.

One more win and they would be in the championship game.

The JV team's next match was against K. L. Enron Middle School, "Home of the Screaming Bulls." Their players all must have had bad colds with stuffed-up noses because my skunk smell did not have a deterrent effect like it did in the Blazing Spuds game.

The Screaming Bulls wasted no time moving the ball downfield and taking a shot on our goal.

But in spite of the skunk fiasco, I had gained confidence in the previous match. (Although I kept glancing behind me toward the nearby brush, just in case.)

The Screaming Bulls took three shots on goal and I blocked all three. I even got to do one of those hotshot goalkeeper blocks where the body goes airborne and stretches out from fingers to toes.

Meanwhile, Joey and Stephanie Jennison took turns attacking the Screaming Bulls goal. Joey would steal the ball and dart, quick as a flea, between the opponents' legs and run downfield.

Then he'd kick the ball into the net before the poor goalkeeper even realized that Joey had the ball.

And Stephanie was a master of foot-eye coordination. She controlled a soccer ball with the feet just like a point guard controls a basketball with the hands.

Backward and forward.

Side to side.

Behind her back.

When Stephanie kicked, the ball shot like a line drive. Or she'd put a spin on the ball and it would curve around defenders. Or she'd fake them out and chip-shot the ball over their head to a teammate.

Just before the half, the Screaming Bulls center midfielder took the ball away from Liz Casey and dribbled straight for our goal. Joey easily caught up to him and slid like a baseball player and knocked the ball away.

The ball rolled toward our goal and into the penalty area, which meant that I could sprint out and intercept the ball with my hands just like a defensive back in football. But the Screaming Bulls player recovered from Joey's deflection and raced toward the ball.

I had a split second to decide: Do I stay back and try to block a kick, or do I run out and try to grab the ball before the opponent can make a kick?

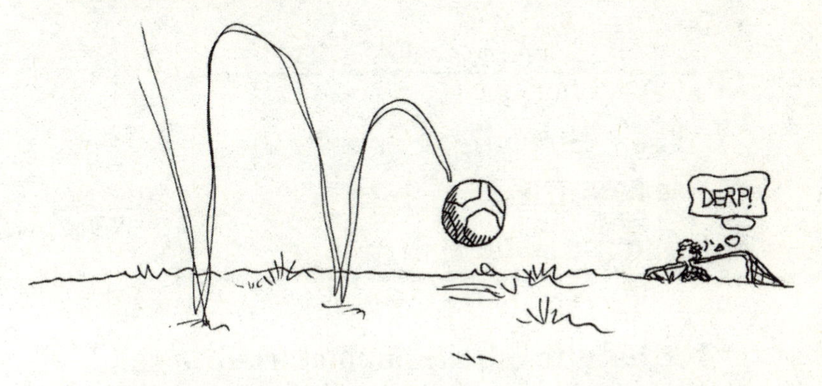

You already know that I have quick feet. No brag. It's just a fact.

So I sprinted out, leaving the goal unprotected, and fell on top of the ball. The Screaming Bulls player had to slam on the brakes and dive over the top of me to avoid a foul.

It was a risky move, but I saved a goal.

The referee blew the whistle for the half. The score was tied.

We jogged off the field to suck on orange segments. My teammates shouted, at a safe distance from my skunk odor, "Nice save!"

And Coach K gave me what most sports experts consider the ultimate compliment from a coach.

It's hard to admit, but I started to think that maybe I was wrong about the game of soccer.

Soccer wasn't boring. Even though there wasn't a lot scoring like in basketball (except in matches where Thunderfoot was on the field), there was a lot of action—especially for a goalkeeper like me.

And it's true that soccer players run up

and down the field with very few breaks unless you keel over from a broken leg or some other ailment, but I realized that's part of the excitement. At any given moment, there was a one-on-one matchup where one player was trying to move the ball and a defender was trying to stop him.

(But probably not with a bulldozer.)

Oh, and those yellow or red cards the ref pulls out when there is a foul? Well, I still wished they would just signal with their hands like in basketball or football.

We lost the match with the Screaming Bulls.

In the second half, they repeatedly moved the ball into scoring position. But each time, the kick was stopped by me or a teammate.

My confidence continued to soar. I even started to believe that I might have a future as a goalkeeper in the most popular game in the universe.

There were about five seconds left in the match, when something extraordinary happened.

The ball landed in front of our goal. Joey and Stephanie were there to control the ball. One of them easily could have moved in and kicked the ball out of scoring range. But the two best players on our team made a critical error.

They hesitated.

A Screaming Bulls player did not hesitate and charged in. I didn't stand a chance. She slammed the ball past my outreached hands and into the corner of the goal.

Game over.

Joey and Stephanie stood frozen in place staring at each other.

The Mighty Plumbers JV team was done.

Meanwhile, the varsity team smeared A. E. Neuman Middle School ("Home of the Madmen") in the semifinal match, one goal to zip.

The game was tied until the final seconds. The Spiro players were moving the ball according to Coach Earwax's designed plays, but they never got it into the goal.

The whole time, Mr. Jimerino was screaming his lungs out telling Jimmy to ignore the designed play and do it on his own.

Jimmy stuck with Coach Earwax's plan until he could no longer ignore his dad's screaming.

He dribbled the ball the length of the field, without passing off even once, and he scored the winning goal, which made Mr. Jimerino very happy.

Becky and Ricky and Jimmy and his kiss-up posse were headed into the tournament championship game.

They would be playing Thunderfoot and Nike Prep. The Fighting Platypuses had pretty much annihilated the highly ranked Steaming Omelets of Les Bois Middle School, a hundred to zip.

When I got back to the hotel, I stripped out of my stanky soccer gear and tossed the jersey, shorts, socks—even my underwear—into the garbage chute at the end of the hallway.

I climbed into the shower and drenched myself for about two hours. And I'm not even exaggerating.

But after all of the hot water and soap and scrubbing, my body still smelled like skunk. I think it was stuck deep down in the pores of my skin.

That night, Carlos got to sleep comfortably in the bed instead of on the couch because I was banished from the room.

The next morning at the delicious Laurensville Garden Hotel buffet breakfast, Thunderfoot and Becky O'Callahan were sitting at the same table. They both had plates piled high with waffles, bacon, eggs, sausage, hash browns, and biscuits.

I was thinking maybe they were doing some kind of research in advance of the Big Game. Like maybe the hotshot Spiro player and the hotshot Nike Prep player were checking each other out, searching for some kind of mental weakness in their opponent.

Or maybe they were just sharing a table and eating a delicious buffet breakfast.

Jimmy Jimerino was sitting two tables away. He did not approve of Becky socializing with a player from the team that Spiro would face in the championship game. He and his posse kept staring over at Thunderfoot and whispering among themselves.

At one point, Thunderfoot looked over at Jimmy and his kiss-up posse and smiled.

Jimmy and his posse were flabbergasted. They were not expecting Thunderfoot's purely friendly greeting.

The championship game of the Laurensville Invitational Soccer Tournament attracted a gigantic crowd.

The sidelines and both ends of the field were jam-packed with spectators. There were coaches and players from other teams and every type of parent—Hunky-Dories, Howlers, and Buttinskies.

Even though Thunderfoot was still in middle school, several scouts from professional soccer teams showed up at the match to check out the legendary kid from Brazil.

Soccer scouts are very secretive. They all were cleverly disguised as ordinary spectators so they could covertly take notes about Thunderfoot's amazing martial-arts soccer abilities without tipping off the competition.

Jimmy Jimerino's dad had arrived at the field four hours before the match so he could seize the prime spot on the sideline at midfield and set up the folding chair that he would never sit in.

Joey, Carlos, and I once again sat on top of the nearby grassy hill to get away from the crowd. It was practically like sitting on the bench, so my friends and I felt right at home.

There was just one problem. I was no longer bothered by the skunk odor—sort of like when you have bad breath but it only bothers other people.

But Joey and Carlos still insisted on a strict boundary, although I wasn't forced to sit quite as far away as before.

Down on the field, the Fighting Platypuses marched like robots onto the field for warm-ups. It's a Nike Prep tradition, both strange and awesome. They paraded in a circle and chanted their team motto:

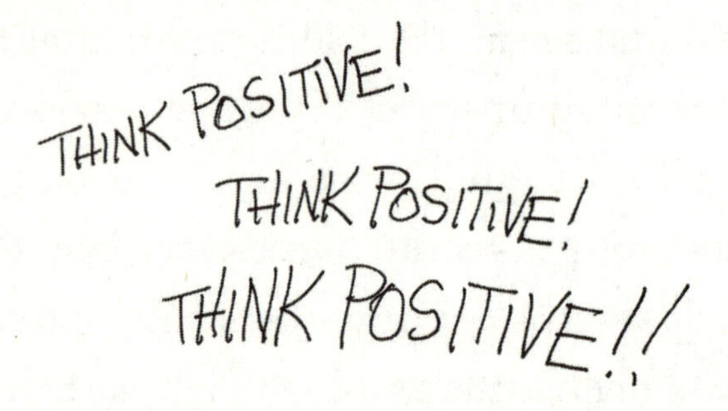

Meanwhile, the Mighty Plumbers stretched out and loosened up in silence.

I couldn't tell if they were just trying to focus their minds on the game or if they were nervous about playing a team that had won every soccer match in the tournament by a hundred to zip.

• • •

Spiro took the kickoff at midfield to start the match. Jimmy tapped the ball to Becky, and she dribbled forward.

After a few yards, Thunderfoot moved in to defend against Becky.

We couldn't hear it from way up on the hill, but Dewey Taylor later told me that Thunderfoot smiled and tried to greet Becky in his usual manner.

"Good day, sun . . ."

But it was game time, and Becky was all business.

She pulled a spectacular spin move and dribbled around Thunderfoot. He just stood there, dumbfounded.

Becky dribbled the ball up the middle of the field, weaving through defenders, and kicked the ball into the goal—even though Mr. Jimerino was yelling his lungs out telling Becky to pass Jimmy the ball so *he* could score.

Mighty Plumbers one, Fighting Platypuses zip.

After Becky scored, she jogged back to the Spiro end of the field, and Thunderfoot said something to her as she passed by—probably "Good day, sunshine!"

My friends and I started thinking that Thunderfoot and the Platypuses were overrated and the Mighty Plumbers would pull off a major upset.

Wrongity, wrong, wrong.

Thunderfoot got down to business.

The polite guy from Brazil stole the ball from Spiro players pretty much whenever he wanted. Then Thunderfoot used his practically superhuman skills to rip through the Spiro defenders and blast the ball into the goal.

Somewhere, hidden among the spectators, the soccer scouts were probably scribbling like madmen into their secret notebooks.

But it wasn't just Thunderfoot who scored goals. He passed off to his Nike Prep teammates—even when he was wide open—and they joined in the slaughter.

Ricky couldn't stop Thunderfoot. Becky couldn't stop him. And Jimmy couldn't even get close enough to *try* to stop him.

Thunderfoot was unstoppable.

Poor Ricky tried hard to block the kicks, but all he could do was get a hand on the ball as it blazed into the goal. Thunderfoot's kicks were so powerful, the referee had to stop the match and replace the goal net.

While the Nike Prep fans cheered and clapped, the Spiro fans all sat silently in their folding chairs—all except one.

Mr. Jimerino was driven right out of his skull.

He paced the sideline as if he was the coach.

He screamed at Jimmy for standing like a dead tree. He yelled at the referee for not calling "obvious" fouls on Thunderfoot. And he shouted at Becky and the other Spiro players.

It was more painful to watch Mr. Jimerino blow his head gasket than it was to watch the slaughter happening on the field.

The half ended with Nike Prep ahead, 60–1.

I don't know why, but watching a slaughter like that created a powerful hunger. So Joey, Carlos, and I decided to grab a quick snack before the slaughter continued in the second half.

The concession stand food at the tournament was nowhere near as good as the excellent food at Goodfellow Stadium. (Not a commercial endorsement!) But there were a few tasty items.

Joey lucked out. They had fresh churros

smothered in sugar, pretty much his all-time favorite snack. Carlos bought an organic spinach-and-kale salad with balsamic vinaigrette.

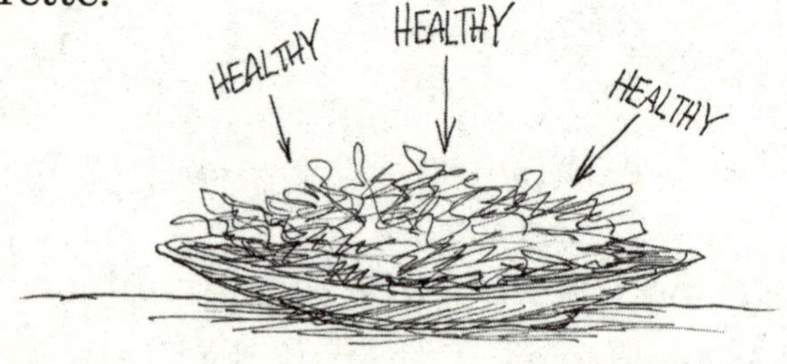

Why? I don't know. You'd have to ask Carlos.

I bought two large bean burritos, a bag of jalapeño tortilla chips, and a banana-chocolate slushy. Normally, I would only get one burrito, but I didn't eat much at breakfast because I was too busy watching Becky and Thunderfoot annoy Jimmy and his kiss-up posse.

By the time we got back on the hill, I had finished one burrito and was halfway through the second one.

On the field, the players were loosening up for the second half, but I noticed that Ricky

Schnauzer was on the sideline talking with Coach Earwax, Coach K, and Tony Fitz, the team athletic trainer. They were examining Ricky's hands.

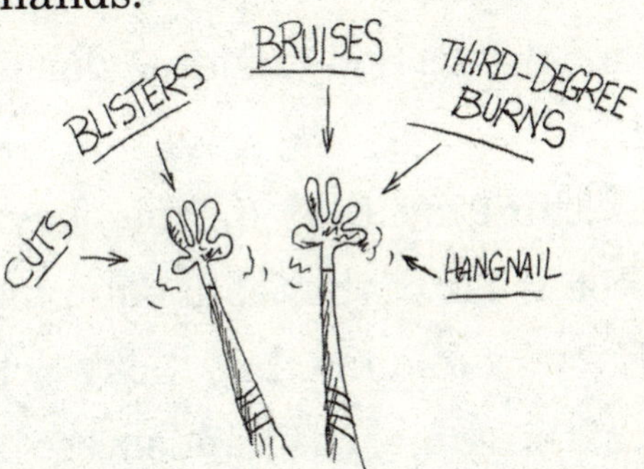

I saw Tony shake his head no, and then Ricky walked over to the bench and sat down.

I had just slurped up the last drop of my banana-chocolate slushy when Coach K turned and looked up the hill. She pointed toward me and then Coach Earwax motioned for me to come down to the sideline.

I did one of those "who, me?" things, thinking maybe they were summoning Joey. Or maybe Carlos.

More likely Joey.

But they were pointing at me!

I scarfed the last of my jalapeño tortilla chips and jogged down to the sideline. My "quick snack" jostled up and down in my stomach.

I was thinking that maybe they needed me to keep track of the team equipment. But Coach Earwax told me that Ricky Schnauzer was out of the game. His hands were blistered and bruised from Thunderfoot's relentless barrage.

I was so shocked, a belch rolled up my throat and shoved some banana-chocolate slushy out of my nose.

Coach Earwax had no backup goalkeeper. He "borrowed" me from the JV team.

I needed a uniform, so Ricky and I dashed into the restroom and swapped clothing. His uniform fit just right on me, but his soccer shoes were a size too big.

Poor Ricky got the worse end of the trade. The pores of my skin had leaked skunk stank onto the clothes that I gave him.

I joined the other Spiro players on the

field. Becky spotted me and she sort of smiled, but not quite Nature's Near-Perfect Smile. Jimmy spotted me and he pinched the bridge of his nose as if he had a sudden splitting headache.

On the sideline, Mr. Jimerino screamed his lungs out at Coach Earwax.

I only had enough time to do one stretch before the match resumed. I tried to touch my toes, but my belly was stuffed full of burritos and chips and slushy, so I could only reach my ankles.

Before I took my position in front of the

goal, Coach Earwax handed me a spare set of gloves. He apologized because it was the only gloves left. Apparently, Thunderfoot's kicks had destroyed *three* pairs of Ricky's gloves.

The second half began with Nike Prep kicking off.

They wasted no time resuming what would become known in Spiro T. Agnew folklore as the Great Thunderfoot Massacre.

I won't tell you that I stopped every one of Thunderfoot's kicks on goal because that would be a gigantic whopper. But I did stop all of his teammates' goal attempts.

They came in fast and furious. Thunderfoot

would move the ball in and out of the Spiro defenders and then pass off to a wide-open teammate.

I dove left, right, up, down on my belly and blocked all of those shots on goal. I started thinking that I could stop the massacre. But then Thunderfoot would slam a kick right through my hands.

The constant barrage was wearing me down. The burritos and chips and slushy made my stomach feel as if I had swallowed a bowling ball. My gloves were getting ripped apart by Thunderfoot's kicks. My hands were blistered and bruised. And my feet were slipping around in Ricky's shoes that were a size too big.

But I did have one thing going for me.

[SKUNK = STANK]

Because of all the stress, I started to sweat like a hotshot athlete. The pores of my skin opened up like faucets and out gushed a huge plume of gnarly, stanky skunk odor.

The Nike Prep players, including Thunderfoot, started avoiding the Odor Zone near our goal.

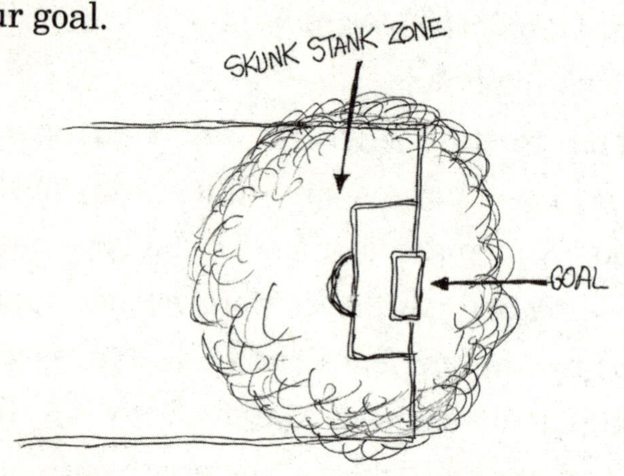

It was like an invisible defense shield.

Meanwhile, the Spiro players never gave up trying to make the Great Thunderfoot Massacre less of a massacre.

Becky and Jimmy would drive the ball down close to the Platypuses goal and take a shot, but Thunderfoot would fly in out of nowhere every time and either block the shot or steal the ball.

Mighty Plumbers were running around trying as hard as they could to score a goal and stop Thunderfoot from scoring.

At one point, Skinny Dennis collapsed and sprawled out on the turf, motionless, right in front of the Spiro goal. The ref actually stopped the match, a rarity in soccer. Coach Earwax and Tony Fitz, the athletic trainer, had to pick Skinny up and carry him off the field.

Players, coaches, and spectators were concerned, but Skinny Dennis didn't suffer some kind of hideous injury or get bit by a blood-sucking mosquito.

He was just overcome by my skunk fumes.

Nike Prep was ahead, 99–1, with about ten seconds left in the match.

The high scores that Nike Prep had racked up in the tournament were unprecedented in the game of soccer—at least as far as I could tell. And the Mighty Plumbers had a chance to do what no other team in the tournament could do: hold the Platypuses to under one hundred points.

With time ticking down, Thunderfoot once

again dribbled the ball downfield. He worked the ball in and out of Spiro defenders until he was close to our goal.

On the sideline, Mr. Jimerino screamed at his son.

Jimmy Jimerino put up one last stand against Thunderfoot.

He rushed in and tried to kick the ball away, but Thunderfoot kept control. Then he circled—*circled*—Jimmy. Around and around, just toying with him.

Jimmy finally got so frustrated, he charged in like a linebacker and tackled Thunderfoot!

It was an excellent tackle that would get cheers and applause in football, but all it gets you in soccer is a foul and a trip to the bench. The referee immediately gave Jimmy the red card, and he was kicked out of the match.

On the sideline, Mr. Jimerino erupted. The Howler-Buttinsky screamed his lungs out at the referee.

He accused Thunderfoot of faking the linebacker tackle. Derp!

The referee finally had enough of Mr. Jimerino. He pulled out a red card and kicked Mr. Jimerino off the sideline—the first time in the entire history of the Laurensville Invitational Soccer Tournament that a parent had gotten the boot.

Mr. Jimerino grabbed his folding chair that he never sat in and stormed off the sideline. As he left, the rest of the spectators erupted in cheers.

Mr. Jimerino went into exile. He walked a short distance away from the field and sat down in his folding chair on a nearby hill.

Because Jimmy's foul happened in the penalty zone, the Platypuses were awarded a penalty kick. It would be one-on-one.

Thunderfoot kicking.

Me defending.

The referee set the ball for the penalty kick twelve yards in front of the goal. Thunderfoot lined up and waited.

I quickly ditched my tattered gloves and put on the fresh pair. Then I sat down and pulled off Ricky's cleats because my feet were blistered from sliding around in sweaty shoes that were a size too big.

I moved into position in the middle of the goal and looked out at Thunderfoot. He was smiling.

Thunderfoot pointed at my bare feet, then at his own bare feet.

I think he took it as a sign of mutual respect because I removed my shoes, but Thunderfoot didn't know about the blisters.

The referee blew his whistle. The one-on-one penalty kick was on.

I'm pretty sure everyone expected that Thunderfoot would score. The only question was how much damage the kick would do to the net, my gloves, and my body.

On the sideline, Coach Earwax and Coach K stared out, expecting the worst. Tony Fitz prepared for athletic-trainer emergency first aid.

Up on the hill, Carlos ripped one of his gigantic belches to boost my spirits.

I glanced over at Becky. She looked right back at me and gave a thumbs-up.

Thunderfoot backed away from the ball and prepared for his penalty kick. I crouched down in a goalkeeper penalty kick stance that I had seen in a YouTube video.

Thunderfoot took three steps and reared back to kick the ball.

I didn't have time to think. I just reacted.

Thunderfoot kicked the ball with his bare foot and I dove to the right. My body went airborne, horizontal to the ground. I stretched out from my fingers to my toes.

The ball slammed into my gloves, but it didn't blow right through and into the net. I grabbed the ball and stopped the goal.

It was epic!

No brag. It's just a fact.

For a moment, the spectators and players were silent. I think they were waiting to see if my hands would burst into flames.

Thunderfoot broke the silence.

The crowd erupted in cheers—even the Nike Prep supporters. I was swarmed by teammates. They jumped up and down and slapped high fives and bumped fists until my skunk fumes drove them away.

Our team acted as if we had won the tournament championship, but we were celebrating the fact that we had held Thunderfoot and Nike Prep to under one hundred points.

The real champions got their trophy and posed for a team photo. Then the professional soccer scouts emerged from hiding and surrounded Thunderfoot. They tried to persuade him to quit school and turn pro and become a billionaire.

But that wasn't going to happen.

Nike Prep's athletic director stepped in. Jeeves pulled Thunderfoot away from the professional soccer scouts. Thunderfoot's parents back in Brazil would not approve.

After escaping the soccer scouts, Thunderfoot ran over to me and tried to shake my hand or give me a high five. I held up both palms and showed him the bruises and blisters from trying to stop his thunder kicks.

I said it was okay and that my hands didn't hurt too much, which was a gigantic whopper. Instead of a high five or shaking hands, we bumped fists. Then I introduced myself because I wanted to know more about him. Especially, I wanted to know his real name. It went like this:

"My name is Steve. Steve Moore."

"My name is Gabriel. Gabriel Thunder-foot."

Whoa. It wasn't just a nickname!

I complimented Gabriel on his amazing abilities in soccer, but he sort of shrugged it off as if he wasn't all that good.

I figured he was just being modest, but Gabriel told me that at home in Brazil his club team is stacked—*stacked*—with hotshot soccer players.

Derp!

Becky caught up to me on the way to the bus for the ride home, but she avoided the Odor Zone.

In spite of the skunk stank, I rustled up nerve and thanked Becky for teaching me to not dislike soccer until I had actually tried it. Then I asked her if we were back to being best friends.

"We're even *better* best friends!"

Whoa!

After that, Ricky and I stopped in a restroom and swapped clothing. I'm pretty sure he took his stanky soccer gear home and burned it.

Before I got on the bus, I saw Mr. Jimerino walking to his car. He was ranting to himself about the "bogus foul" called on Jimmy and his infamous red-card ejection from the sideline.

Mr. Jimerino took a shortcut to the parking lot through some brush and startled the skittish skunk that sprayed me the day before.

The skunk turned his rear end around and let 'er rip. Mr. Jimerino took a direct hit at point-blank range from the skunk's stanky natural defense system.

And I'm not even making that up!

On the ride home, I finally got to sit in a prime shenanigan seat at the very back of the bus. But it wasn't because I shoved past Jimmy and his kiss-up posse and called dibs.

EPILOGUE

So I wasn't exactly a hotshot athlete who shut down Thunderfoot, but I did use my hand-eye coordination and saved *one* of his shots on goal, which no other goalkeeper was able to do.

(I almost said, "I wasn't great, but at least I didn't stink!" But that would have been a gigantic whopper.)

Most importantly, I was now even *better* best friends with the girl who has Nature's

Near-Perfect Smile.

Anyway, I don't even want to be a hotshot athlete. Even though I actually got to play in the soccer tournament, I would have been okay with sitting on the pine.

I'm probably better at it than anyone else my age in the entire universe. End of the bench. Middle of the bench. Doesn't matter.

I'm King of the Bench!

No brag. It's just a fact.

ABOUT THE AUTHOR

STEVE MOORE is a rookie author, amateur cartoonist, and C+ student at Spiro T. Agnew Middle School.

When his rear end isn't glued to the bench beside his two best friends, Joey Linguini and Carlos Diaz, Steve likes to spend time selling sports memorabilia at inflated prices and hanging out with his pets—especially Fido, a large snake who struggles with separation anxiety.

Steve does *not* like to spend time eating broccoli, running wind sprints until his lungs explode, or climbing into the attic to dispose of dead rats.

He lives with his former hotshot athlete dad and turbo-hyper-worrywart mom in the extraordinarily average city of Goodfellow, which may or may not show up on Google Maps.